Storybook Treasury for

Boys

STORYBOOK TREASURY FOR BOYS published in 2003 by Grosset & Dunlap.

ALL ABOARD FIRE TRUCKS: Text copyright © 1991 by Teddy Slater. Illustrations copyright © 1991 by Tom LaPadula.
ALL ABOARD AIRPLANES: Text copyright © 1994 by Grosset & Dunlap. Illustrations copyright © 1994 by George Guzzi.
ALL ABOARD CARS: Text copyright © 1996 by Catherine Daly Weir. Illustrations copyright © 1996 by Courtney.
COWBOYS: Text copyright © 1996 by Lucille Recht Penner. Illustrations copyright © 1996 by Ben Carter.
PIRATES: Text copyright © 1997 by Dina Anastasio. Illustrations copyright © 1997 by Donald Cook.
CONSTRUCTION TRUCKS: Text copyright © 1998 by Grosset & Dunlap. Illustrations copyright © 1998 by Courtney.

All rights reserved. Published by Grosset & Dunlap, a division of Penguin Young Readers Group,
345 Hudson Street, New York, NY, 10014.
GROSSET & DUNLAP is a trademark of Penguin Group (USA) Inc. Published simultaneously in Canada. Printed in the U.S.A.

Library of Congress Cataloging-in-Publication Data is available.

ISBN 0-448-43338-9   A B C D E F G H I J

Storybook Treasury for Boys

By Dina Anastasio, Jennifer Dussling, Frank Evans, Lucille Recht Penner,
Teddy Slater, and Catherine Daly Weir

Illustrated by Ben Carter, Donald Cook, Courtney,
George Guzzi, and Tom LaPadula

GROSSET & DUNLAP

Table of Contents

CONSTRUCTION TRUCKS

By Jennifer Dussling
Illustrated by Courtney

Welcome to a construction site! Nothing is happening here yet, but someone has bought this land and drawn up plans for a house. Soon it will be filled with construction trucks. A year from now, a house will stand right here, and a family will be living in it.

First, bulldozers clear the site for the new house. A bulldozer's heavy steel blade rips boulders out of the ground. A bulldozer doesn't have wheels like a truck or a car. Instead, it has tracks like a tank. The thick, rubber treads on the tracks help the bulldozer grip rough earth and also can keep it from sinking in soft mud.

Sometimes a bulldozer has a ripper on the back, like this one. A ripper looks like a giant tooth. It tears through hard ground.

After the bulldozer clears away rocks and trees, equipment is brought in to dig a hole in the ground. This hole is for the foundation, the support structure of the building. The foundation also will be the house's basement.

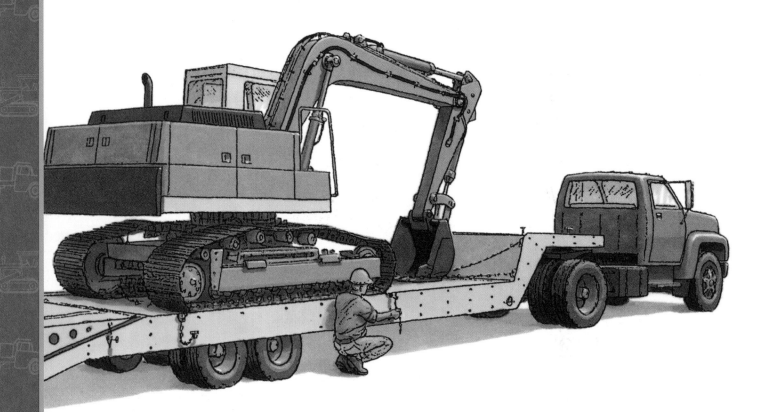

With the bucket at the end of its long metal arm, a backhoe cuts deep trenches in the ground and scoops out loads of dirt. Like a bulldozer, the backhoe has two tracks instead of wheels. The upper part of a backhoe swivels around over the tracks. It can dig on any side, or dig on one side and dump on the other.

A payloader helps the backhoe dig the hole for the foundation. The payloader pushes through dirt, collects it in its wide bucket, raises the load up, and drops it in a dump truck.

A backhoe loader is a cross between a backhoe and a payloader. It has a backhoe on one end and a payloader on the other!

The backhoe and payloader fill the dump truck with dug-up dirt and rock. Dump trucks are very strong. A small dump truck, like this one, carries about a ton of dirt, but a large dump truck can hold more than 100 tons—that's like carrying seventeen elephants!

Rolling on large, rugged tires, the dump truck takes the dirt
and rock away from the construction site. When the truck gets
to its unloading spot, its back end tilts up so the load can slide off.

When the hole for the foundation is finished, a concrete mixer pours the walls and the floor of the basement. The back of the concrete mixer looks like a barrel on its side that turns around and around without stopping. Why does the back of the truck keep turning? Concrete is a mixture of cement, sand, and gravel that hardens as it dries. By turning around and around, the barrel keeps the concrete from hardening on the way to the building site.

Carpenters take over after the concrete for the foundation is poured. They build the walls, the floors, and the roof with tools like saws and hammers and drills. But the owner of the house has one more idea that needs a very special truck. She wants to move a big tree from her old house to this new one.

The four steel blades of a tree spade burrow under the tree and lift it out, roots and all. The tree is brought to the new house, and the tree spade lowers the tree into a hole it has already dug. The tree will look like it's always been there!

Here is a different kind of construction site. A new road is going to run through this area. Which trucks are used to make a road?

After a bulldozer clears away small trees and bushes, a motor grader comes through. The motor grader has a long blade mounted on its underside. This blade drags over the ground, leveling it and smoothing it out. Soon the ground is flat enough to pave.

Some roads are made of concrete, but this road will be asphalt.
Asphalt is a mixture of cement and crushed stone or sand.

Workers lay down the asphalt with a paving truck. Then a roller rolls over the pavement, making it smooth and hard. After traffic lines are painted, the road is ready for cars!

In a city, a wall of wooden boards hides another construction site. No trees and boulders have to be removed from this site, but there is one thing still to be cleared—another building! This old parking garage will be torn down to make room for a new office building—a skyscraper.

PARK
HOUR · DAY
WEEK
RATES

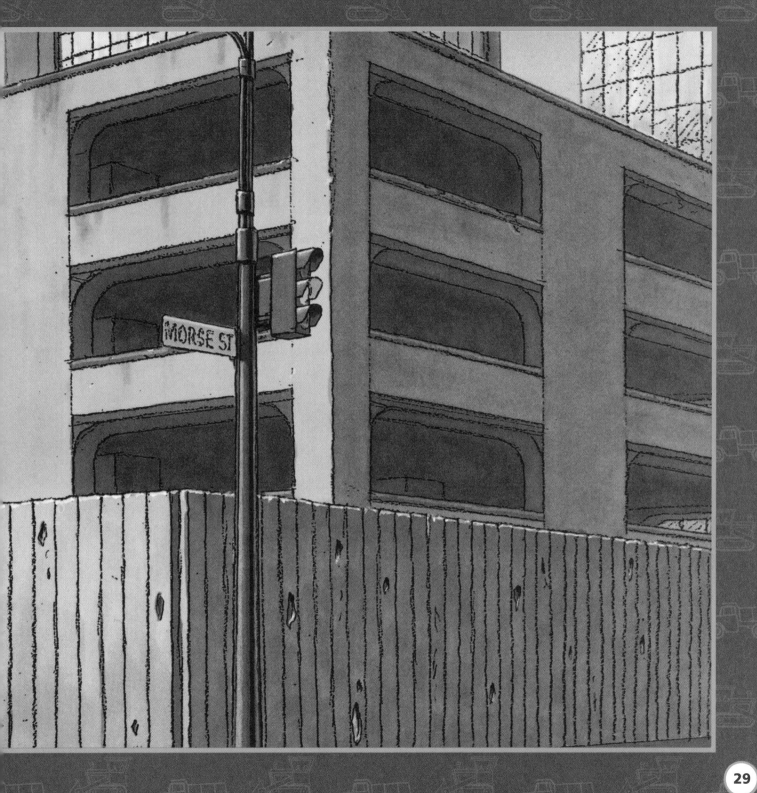

How will they knock down a big building like this parking garage? First, a wrecking ball is attached to a ground crane. The crane swings the huge steel ball against the walls of the garage, smashing them to pieces. Trucks with hammer attachments break up floors and pavements. Some construction workers also use jackhammers to break apart the smaller pieces.

Backhoes dig a foundation for the new skyscraper. Then a pile driver is brought in. A pile driver hammers long steel posts into the ground, deeper and deeper, until the posts, called piles, hit hard rock. Piles spread the weight of the heavy building so that the ground and rock support it. Sometimes piles go as far down as 200 feet!

The frame of the skyscraper is already ten stories high. How do the workmen get building materials, like steel girders, up that high? They use a crane.

With its huge, strong hook, a crane lifts heavy girders and beams and sets them in place. When two cranes are needed, sometimes one crane will lift the other crane to a higher floor. Construction workers call this "jumping" the cranes.

A concrete mixer can't reach above the first floor of a skyscraper. That's why there is a special machine that carries concrete to the higher floors. It is called a concrete pump.

The concrete is taken to the construction site in a concrete mixer. Then the mixer pours the concrete into the back of the concrete pump. The pump forces the concrete up its long pipe. When the last bit of concrete is poured, the workers have a "topping out" ceremony. That means the skyscraper is finished!

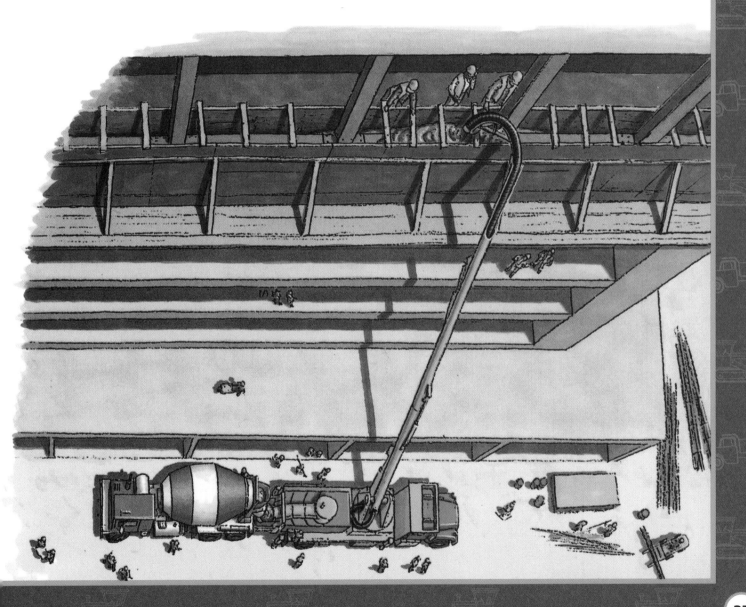

Hundreds of years ago, people had to build houses and buildings using just handheld tools. We're so lucky to have construction trucks today to help with the big jobs!

All Aboard
FIRE TRUCKS

By Teddy Slater • Illustrated by Tom LaPadula

*C*lang, clang, clang! Here come the fire fighters to put out the fire. There are only two groups of fire trucks—pumpers and ladders. But in each group there are many different kinds of trucks, and each truck has its own very special job to do.

PUMPER

Pumpers

The first trucks to reach the fire are the pumpers. The fire fighters on these trucks must spray water on the fire as quickly as possible. They often hose off nearby buildings as well, to keep the flames from spreading.

The pumper carries its own tanks of water and many hoses and nozzles to draw even more water from hydrants. But the most important piece of equipment on this truck is a pump. The pump boosts the pressure of the water so it comes out of the hoses in a strong and steady stream.

MINIPUMPER

A small pumper is called a minipumper. Although it can't carry as much water as a large pumper, this little vehicle does a very big job in crowded cities. The minipumper speeds down narrow city streets way ahead of all the other trucks. By the time it has used up its own water, the other trucks will have arrived at the fire.

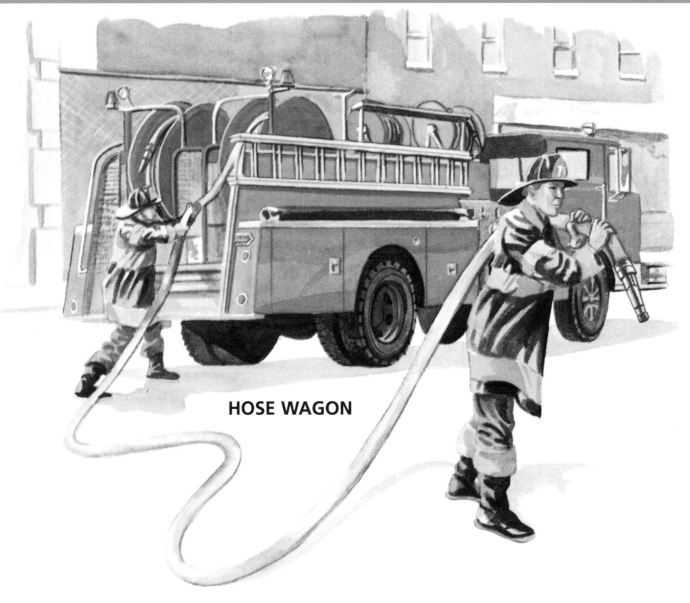

HOSE WAGON

The hose wagon is seen only at the biggest fires, where extra hoses may be needed. This truck carries many hoses and nozzles, as well as fire extinguishers, first-aid equipment, and its own supply of water in a booster tank.

FIREBOAT

The fireboat is one pumper that doesn't carry a drop of water on board. It doesn't have to—it can draw all it needs directly from the lake, river, or ocean it patrols. Fireboats are used to fight fires on piers, in waterfront buildings, and on other ships.

OINT JARROW FIRE DEPARTMENT

Oil and chemical fires cannot be put out with water. The foam unit fights these fires with a special liquid that comes out looking like soapsuds. One generator on a small truck can make enough foam to fill a gymnasium. Although foam cannot be sprayed high into the air like water, it is very useful for putting out basement or ground-level fires.

FOAM UNIT

This foam truck is specially designed for fires in tall oil tanks. It has a long boom with a nozzle at the top. When fire fighters raise the boom, the foam can be poured over the tank.

FOAM UNIT

CRASH RESCUE VEHICLE

Because airport fires most often involve explosive chemicals and fuels, the crash rescue vehicle, or CRV, also pumps out a thick foam instead of plain water. The foam is sprayed out of two big guns on the roof of the truck.

The crash rescue vehicle coming out of the airport hangar is less than 6 feet tall! It was made to fit into areas with little head room and to clear low hangar entrances. Like most CRVs, it is painted bright yellow so that it can be seen clearly from the air.

The brush truck is used to put out small fires in fields and woods that are called brush fires. That's why it must be tough enough to travel over the most rocky, rugged ground. Because there are no fire hydrants in the country, the brush truck carries a big supply of water and a pump, as well as many hoses, shovels, and rakes.

BRUSH TRUCK

BULLDOZER PUMPER

For large forest fires, the bulldozer pumper carries its own bulldozer along with the usual pump, hose, and water tanks. The bulldozer is used to make a clear path around the burning area, to keep the fire from spreading. The path is called a firebreak.

Ladders

Unlike pumpers, ladder trucks don't carry any water. They carry hooks and other cutting tools to tear down walls and floors so fire fighters can reach people trapped inside a burning building. They also carry ladders to help people escape. That's why these trucks are sometimes called hook-and-ladders.

REAR-MOUNT AERIAL LADDER

The rear-mount aerial ladder has a very long ladder that can be raised more than 100 feet—as high as a ten-story building! The ladder is attached to a motorized turntable on the truck. By simply pushing a button, the fire fighter can make the ladder move in any direction.

The tower ladder has a 150-foot boom that can be mechanically raised and lowered. At the top of the boom is a platform, or bucket, where the fire fighter stands. A built-in hose runs all the way up to the platform so the fire fighter can spray water directly onto the fire. And there's enough room in the bucket for several fire victims to be brought safely down to the ground.

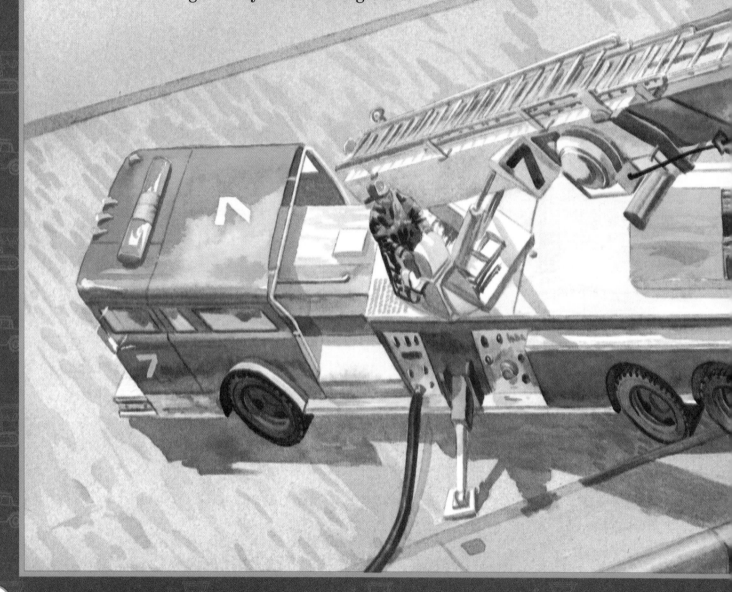

TOWER LADDER

TILLER RIG

The tiller rig is made in two separate pieces so it can turn sharp street corners. The two pieces of the truck are joined together like a tractor trailer, and each part has its own driver. The driver of the front part is called the chauffeur. The one who steers the back part is called the tillerman. The two drivers can use a bell, buzzer, or two-way radio to communicate with each other.

SEARCHLIGHT TRUCK

Auxiliary Vehicles

Auxiliary means "giving help," and that's exactly what the fire department's auxiliary cars and trucks do. They give all the help they can to the engines and ladders that put out the fires.

The sunniest days can seem pitch-black in the midst of a roaring fire. But the searchlight truck helps fire fighters find their way through the thickest, darkest smoke. Even at night, fire fighters can see exactly what they're doing when all the special searchlights on the truck are turned on.

The ambulance is like a mini-medical center on wheels. This vehicle brings cots, stretchers, blankets, oxygen tanks, first-aid kits, and trained attendants to the scene of the fire. Fire victims can be treated inside, or if necessary, they can be rushed to the nearest hospital.

AMBULANCE

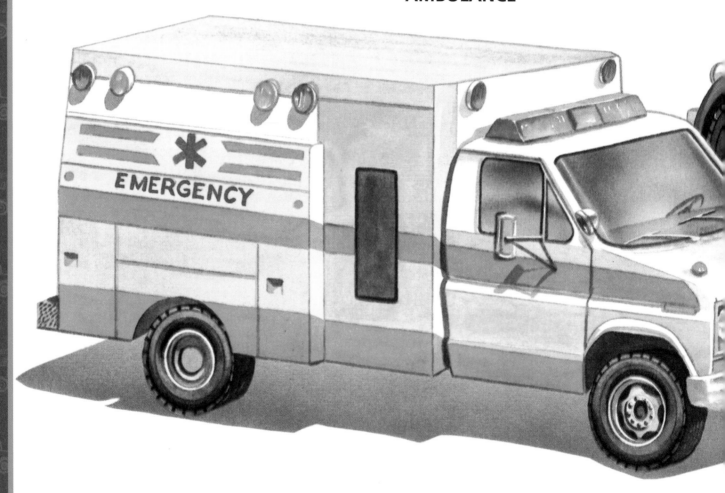

AIR UTILITY WAGON

Fire fighters often wear face masks that are connected to oxygen tanks to help them breathe in very smoky places. If a fire rages too long, the oxygen tanks will eventually become empty. The air utility wagon acts as a refilling station, bringing fresh tanks of air to fire fighters at major fires.

MOBILE HEADQUARTERS UNIT

Big-city fire fighters often need big help—and that's just what they get from these two small trucks.

Inside the mobile headquarters unit are floor plans for all the big buildings in the area. Every door, window, and fire exit is clearly marked on the plans so fire fighters will know the best way to attack the burning building.

HIGH-RISE UNIT

The high-rise unit is filled with special equipment for fighting fires in city skyscrapers. There's a concrete core cutter for breaking through floors, walls, and ceilings, and lots of extra ropes, axes, and ladders.

RESCUE VAN

The fire department's rescue van is on hand for all kinds of emergencies—not only fires. It is equipped with life-saving tools such as inflatable rafts and scuba gear for underwater rescues, hydraulic jacks to lift the heaviest objects, and the Jaws of Life. This powerful tool can slice through the toughest steel and even pry open crushed automobiles to free people trapped inside. The rescue van also carries tow chains, ropes, saws, axes, oxygen tanks, and air masks.

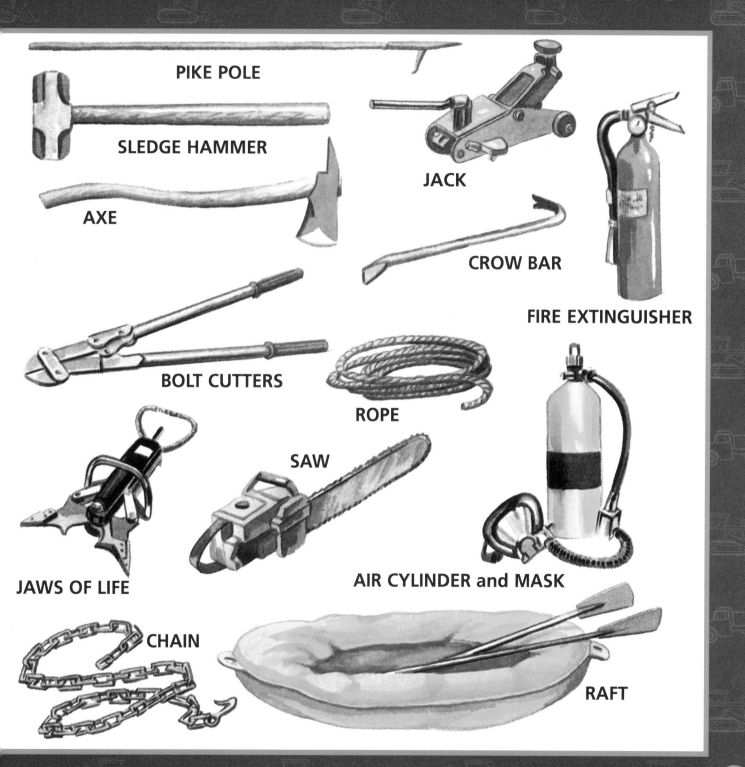

PIKE POLE

SLEDGE HAMMER

JACK

AXE

CROW BAR

FIRE EXTINGUISHER

BOLT CUTTERS

ROPE

JAWS OF LIFE

SAW

AIR CYLINDER and MASK

CHAIN

RAFT

FIRE CHIEF'S CAR

With its red lights flashing and sirens blaring, the fire chief's car races to the biggest fires. The chief has a two-way radio and a car telephone so he can talk to fire fighters at the scene of the fire while he's still on the road. And as soon as the fire is under control, he can give the good news to the people back at the fire station!

All Aboard
CARS

By Catherine Daly Weir
Illustrated by Courtney

There are more than 400 million cars in the world today. They are everywhere—taking people to work, to school, and on vacations. But not so long ago, there were no cars at all. Most people used horses to get where they wanted to go.

The first "horseless carriages," like this Roper Steam Carriage, were powered by steam. They were noisy and dirty and had to stop often to wait for more steam to be made. The coal fires that heated the steam could be dangerous, too!

ROPER STEAM CARRIAGE, 1865

Other early cars, like the Mildé Electric, used electricity to run. Electric cars were clean and quiet, but they were slow and their heavy batteries needed recharging often.

MILDÉ ELECTRIC CAR, 1900

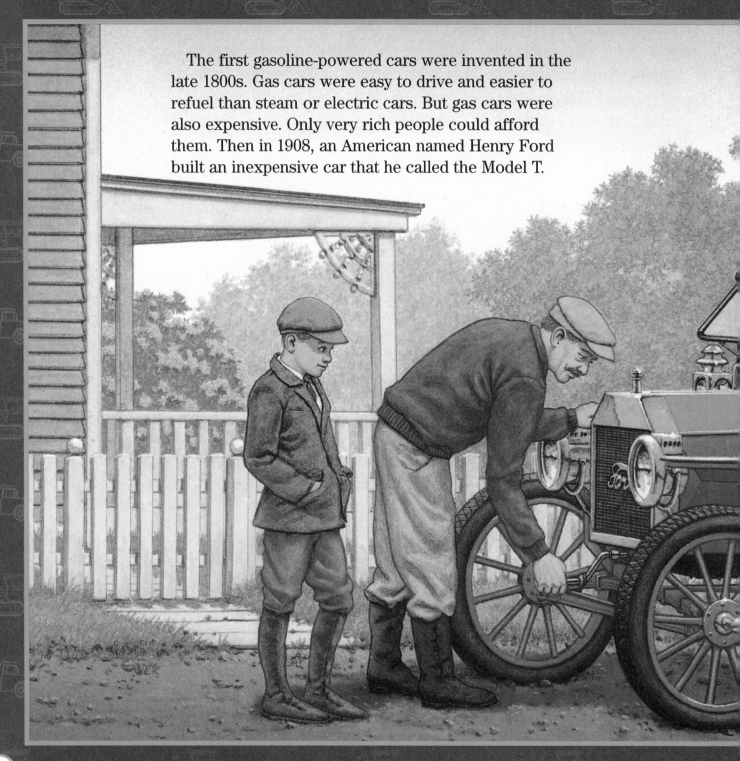

The first gasoline-powered cars were invented in the late 1800s. Gas cars were easy to drive and easier to refuel than steam or electric cars. But gas cars were also expensive. Only very rich people could afford them. Then in 1908, an American named Henry Ford built an inexpensive car that he called the Model T.

The first Model T was small and simple. It did not have bumpers or seat belts or a spare tire. To start the motor, you had to turn a crank, not a key like we do today. But it was a car almost everyone could afford.

FORD MODEL T, 1909

By the 1920s, millions of cars were on the roads. The Bugatti Royale was one of the largest and fanciest "luxury" cars. Like other luxury cars, it was big and comfortable and made for people who wanted to travel in style.

BUGATTI TYPE 41 ROYALE, 1927

MG TC, 1946

For drivers who were more interested in speed, "sports" cars were made. Their powerful engines and smaller, lighter bodies allowed them to go faster than regular cars.

This two-seater MG TC could go as fast as 125 miles per hour. The convertible top and even the front windshield could fold down for open-air driving.

Today, some cars are built just to do special jobs. Most police cars start out as ordinary cars. Then lights and sirens are added. They are used to warn other cars to get out of the way or to tell them to pull over. A screen called a "cage" between the front and back seats holds suspects.

The fire chief has a special car, too. It has lights and a siren so the chief can get to emergencies quickly.

FIRE CHIEF'S CAR

POLICE CAR

A taxicab takes people to places for a fee. Most taxis have a meter that keeps track of how far the cab goes and shows the passenger how much to pay.

TAXICAB

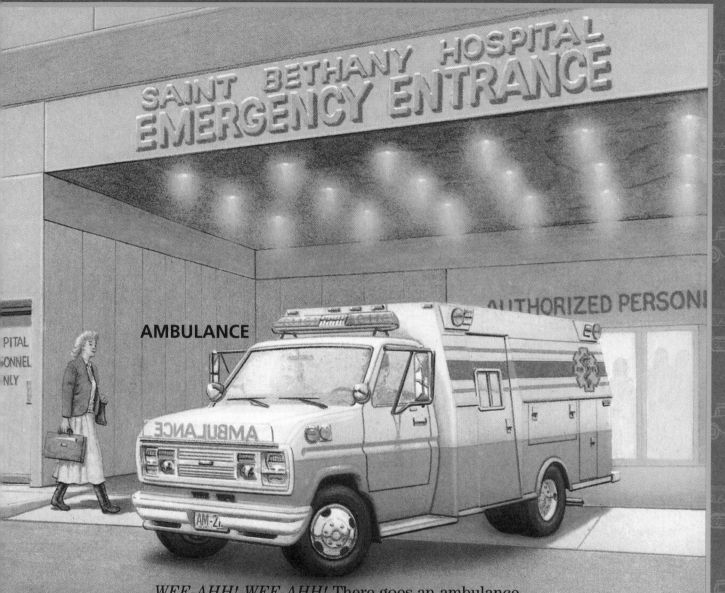

AMBULANCE

WEE-AHH! WEE-AHH! There goes an ambulance. When someone is sick or hurt and needs to get to the hospital fast, an ambulance is called. Ambulances have stretchers, blankets, and other emergency equipment. Some even have teddy bears for young passengers to hold.

U.S. ARMY JEEP, 1941

Jeeps first were used during World War II to help soldiers carry supplies and move from place to place. They can go over rough, bumpy ground that would stop other cars in their tracks. This all-purpose vehicle can even be used as an ambulance in an emergency.

WORLD'S LONGEST LIMOUSINE

Some cars are built just for fun. This custom-built limousine is the longest car in the world. It is 104 feet long—almost as long as three city buses. It even has a putting green!

Some cars are built just to go fast. Race cars are made to be driven by specially trained drivers on specially built tracks. Automobile racing is one of the toughest and most dangerous sports in the world. To protect themselves, drivers wear cushioned helmets, face masks, and fire-resistant clothing—down to their underwear!

There are different kinds of race cars for different kinds of car races. Formula One cars are one type of race car. They ride very low to the ground and have the engine in the rear.

FORMULA ONE CAR

MONACO GRAND PRIX

One of the most glamorous car races of all is the Monaco Grand Prix (grahn PREE). Every spring, Formula One cars drive through the streets of Monte Carlo, the capital of Monaco, at speeds up to 200 miles per hour.

Indy cars look a lot like Formula One racers. But Indy cars are even faster and sturdier. They have to be— Indy races are very long.

The most famous Indy race is the Indianapolis 500, a 500-mile race held on Memorial Day each year. It is one of the fastest car races in the world—and one of the longest. Drivers race around the two-and-a-half-mile track 200 times—in three and a half hours!

INDY CAR

TOP FUEL CAR

Top Fuel Cars, or "Dragsters," race on straight tracks called "strips" that are one-quarter of a mile long. They can reach speeds of more than 260 miles per hour in less than six seconds. Dragsters go so fast they need parachutes to help them stop.

BUDWEISER ROCKET

The fastest car in the world is the three-wheeled Budweiser Rocket. It is thirty-nine feet long and less than two feet wide. Powered by a jet engine, the Budweiser Rocket can go 739 miles per hour—faster than most airplanes can fly!

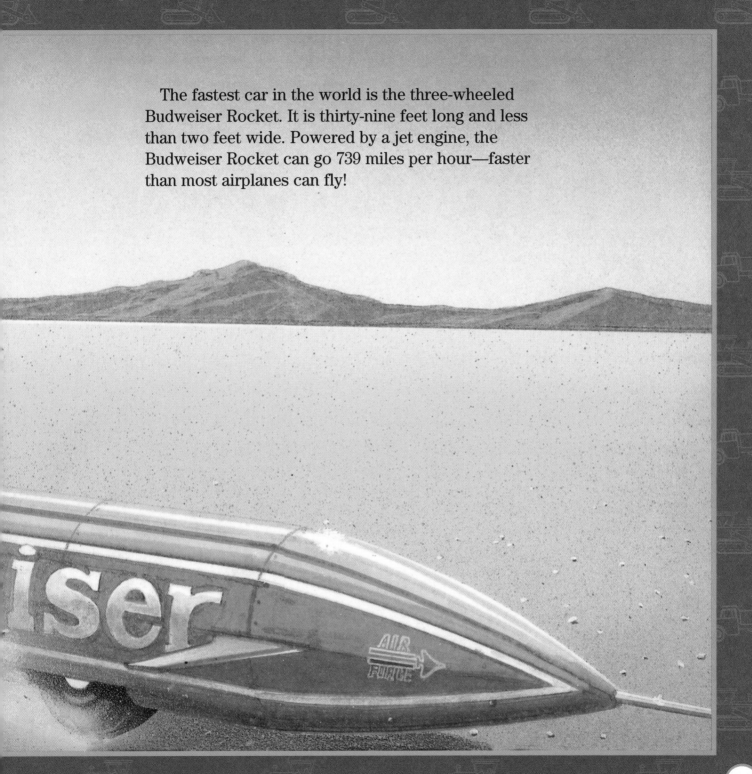

A stock car may look like a regular car, but it sure doesn't drive like one! The engine is taken out and completely rebuilt—or "souped up"—so the car can go more than 200 miles per hour. Because stock cars can reach such dangerously high speeds, a steel frame called a "roll cage" is welded inside. It keeps the roof from collapsing if the car flips over.

STOCK CAR

PIT STOP

The Daytona 500 is a famous stock car race held each year at the Daytona International Speedway in Florida. In long races like the Daytona 500, drivers must pull over for several pit stops. Each car has its own pit and pit crew. The crew cleans the windshield, fills the tank with gas, changes the tires, and makes any needed repairs.

In a car race, every second counts, so pit crews work fast. A smooth pit stop can take as little as fifteen seconds.

SELF-SERVICE GAS STATION

SELF SERVICE

SELF SERVICE

GAS PUMP

A visit to the service station is a lot like a pit stop, only
it doesn't have to happen at lightning speed.

GARAGE

Some gas stations are full-service. The attendant may clean the windshield, check the oil, and fill the gas tank. Other stations are self-service. The customer pumps her own gas. She may want to fill her tires with air, too.

If an oil change, a repair, or a tune-up is needed, the car goes into the garage. It is jacked up on a lift so the mechanic can get a better look.

Car companies are always trying to build better cars—cars that use less gasoline, cars that are safer, and cars that are better for the environment.

Some cars of the future might be solar-powered or run on rechargeable batteries. They might even be able to drive both on land and under water. Who knows what kind of car *you* may be driving someday!

FORD GT90 CONCEPT CAR

All Aboard
AIRPLANES

By Frank Evans
Illustrated by George Guzzi

For thousands of years, people all over the world dreamed of flying. But it wasn't until less than one hundred years ago that someone invented a machine that could really carry people through the air.

On a cold, windy day in 1903, Orville and Wilbur Wright flew the first AIRPLANE ever! The flight lasted only twelve seconds, and went only 120 feet. But it was the beginning of a whole new age of transportation.

Propeller Planes

The first airplanes were powered by propellers. Propellers have blades that spin very fast. The blades push air behind the propeller and make the airplane go forward. Many useful and popular aircraft still use propellers today.

PASSENGER PLANE

The Douglas DC-3 was one of the first popular passenger planes. It began service in 1936 and could carry up to twenty-eight passengers. Many airlines still use them today for short flights.

CROP DUSTER

Some airplanes, like crop dusters, have special jobs. Farmers use crop dusters to spray chemicals on crops to protect the plants from bugs and disease. Flying crop dusters isn't easy. They must be flown slowly and very low to the ground. Sometimes farmers also use these airplanes to sow seeds and spread fertilizer.

FLYING BOAT

The Canadair CL-215 is called a "flying boat." It can take off and land on water as well as on land. It is also used as a "water bomber" for fighting forest fires. In twelve seconds, this airplane can scoop up more than 1,200 gallons of water from a lake or river. The pilot then flies over the fire and dumps the water on it.

The Piper Cub Cheyenne III is a kind of "light" plane. It is used to carry people on short trips. Because this airplane is so easy to fly, it is a favorite of people who fly for fun.

LIGHT PLANE

Helicopters

Helicopters are another kind of aircraft. A rotor on top of the helicopter spins like a propeller to lift the aircraft straight up. Helicopters are slower than airplanes and harder to fly, but they are very useful.

Helicopters can take off and land in small spaces. Because they can go almost anywhere, they are often used during wartime.

Helicopters can hover. This means they can hang in the air in one place. A hovering helicopter can rescue people from sinking ships or burning buildings by dropping the victims a line, then pulling them up.

Helicopters can fly slowly. In big cities, radio and television reporters fly helicopters slowly over highways and warn drivers about any traffic jams they see.

Helicopters can lift and carry things that are too big or heavy for other vehicles to move. The U.S. Army uses the Sikorsky S-64 Skycrane to carry planes, tanks, trucks—and even small buildings!

Jet Planes

Jet planes are another kind of airplane. Powerful jet engines make it possible for these large, heavy planes to fly very far at very high speeds.

JUMBO JET

In 1970, the first "jumbo" jet, the Boeing 747, began service. This giant airliner can carry 500 passengers. It even has six kitchens and twelve bathrooms. The new Boeing 747-400 is even bigger. Today it is the world's largest passenger plane.

The Concorde is a supersonic transport (SST) jet. Supersonic means that the Concorde can go faster than the speed of sound. It is the fastest passenger plane in the world, and can fly all the way from New York to London in three hours. During takeoff and landing, the pilot lowers the Concorde's nose in order to see the runway clearly.

SUPERSONIC JET

This Boeing 727 carries mail instead of people. It looks a lot like a passenger jet, but it has much bigger doors for loading cargo. And because there are no passengers, there is no need for windows. Mail planes are often loaded and flown at night to make sure the mail will be delivered the next day.

MAIL JET

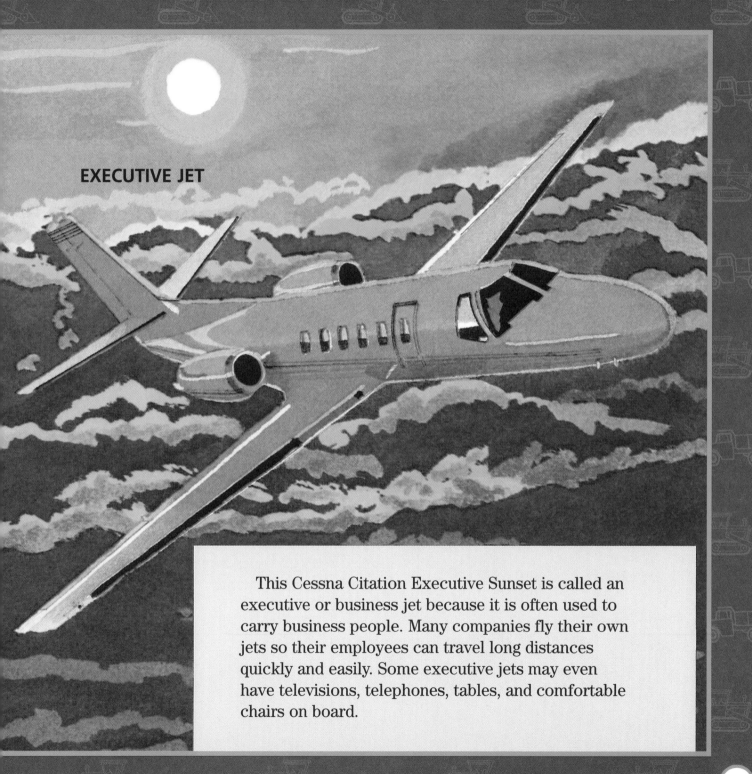

EXECUTIVE JET

This Cessna Citation Executive Sunset is called an executive or business jet because it is often used to carry business people. Many companies fly their own jets so their employees can travel long distances quickly and easily. Some executive jets may even have televisions, telephones, tables, and comfortable chairs on board.

Military Planes

Not all jet planes are made to carry passengers or goods. Many jets are built to be used by the military, during both peacetime and war.

The F-14 Tomcat is one of the U.S. Navy's most popular jet fighters. During takeoffs and landings, the F-14's wings stick straight out to balance the airplane. But for high-speed flying, the wings are moved back. With its wings swept back, the F-14 can fly over two times the speed of sound.

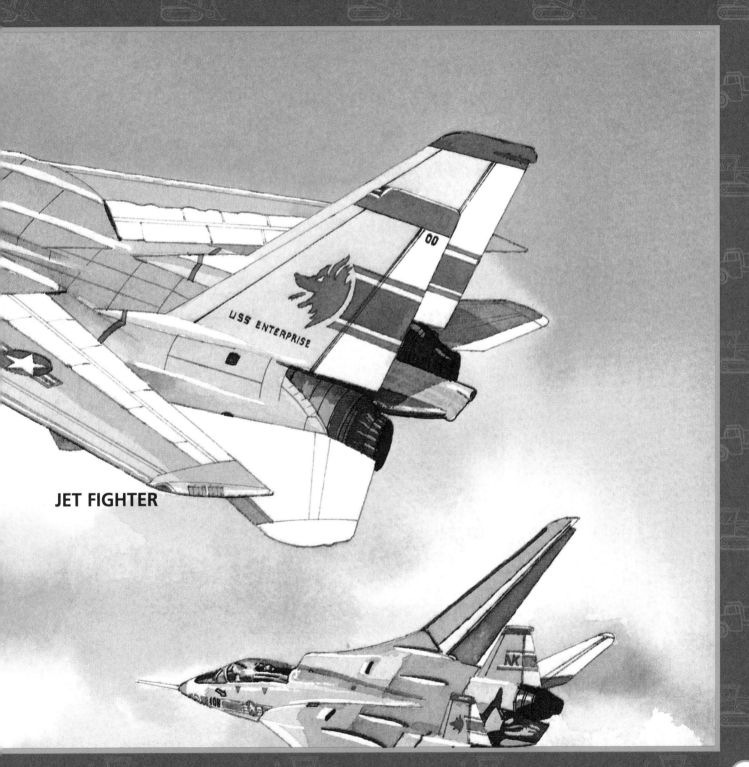

JET FIGHTER

The Lockheed C-5 Galaxy is one of the biggest airplanes in the world. The U.S. Air Force uses it to move tanks and trucks and helicopters, and other large, heavy things that no other aircraft could carry. The Galaxy's nose lifts up to load things that could not fit through the doors of a regular airplane.

CARGO JET

TANKER JET

53135

The U.S. Air Force uses tanker jets, like the KC-135, to refuel other airplanes during flight so the planes won't have to land.

An airplane that needs more fuel flies behind the tanker and hooks up to a tube that pumps the fuel. When the airplane's fuel tanks are full, the tube is pulled up and the airplane falls away to continue on its mission.

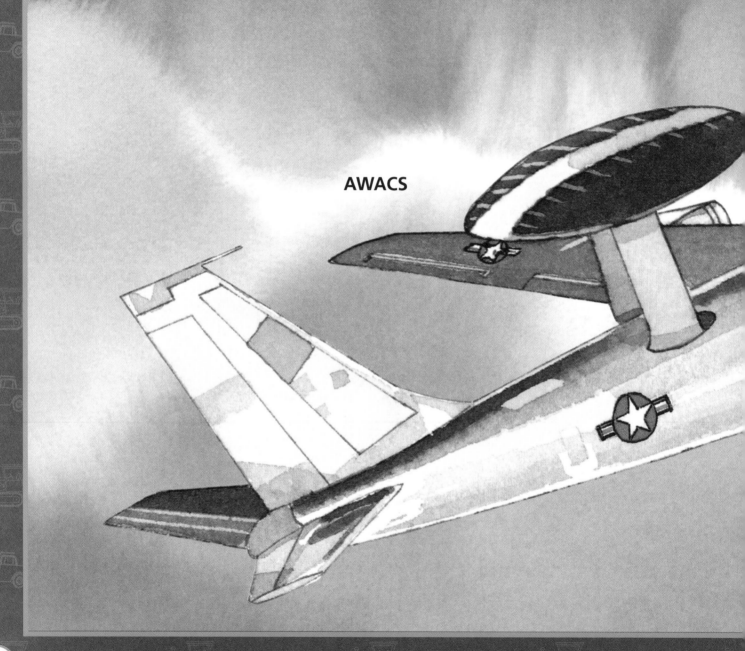

AWACS

The Boeing E-3 Sentry is an AWACS, or Airborne Warning and Control System. This kind of airplane is loaded with high-speed computers and carries powerful antennae on its back so it can communicate with other aircraft, ships, and military bases on the ground. During wartime, an AWACS can serve as a flying command post.

The Lockheed F-117 is a Stealth Fighter. This means it is used to destroy enemy buildings, bridges, and other important targets, without being seen or heard, or detected by radar. The F-117 is specially built to fool radar detectors, and the outside is covered with a special coating that absorbs radar signals. Because the F-117 is flown mostly in the dark of night, it is nicknamed the "Nighthawk."

STEALTH JET

VTOL stands for vertical takeoff and landing. This McDonnell Douglas AV-8B Harrier II VTOL jet takes off and lands straight up and down just like a helicopter, so it can land without runways and even on ships.

But the Harrier flies much faster than a
helicopter—up to 700 miles per hour.
And because of its special jet engines,
the Harrier can even fly backwards.

VTOL

The Space Shuttle is the world's first reusable spacecraft. It takes off from a launching pad like other spacecraft. But after takeoff, the big booster rockets and fuel tanks attached to the shuttle fall away. Then when the Space Shuttle has completed its mission and returns to Earth, it lands on a runway like a regular airplane.

SPACE SHUTTLE

PIRATES

By Dina Anastasio
Illustrated by Donald Cook

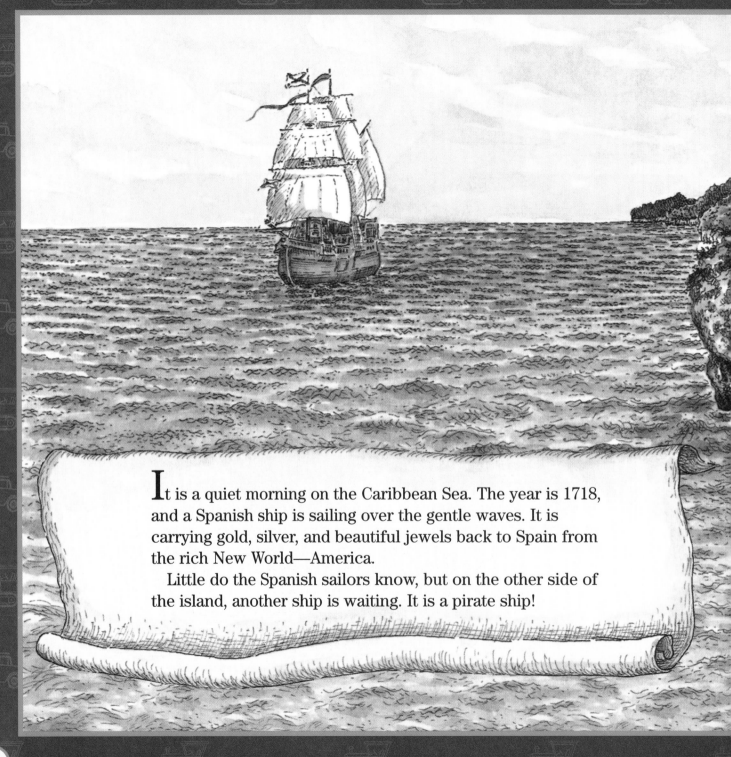

It is a quiet morning on the Caribbean Sea. The year is 1718, and a Spanish ship is sailing over the gentle waves. It is carrying gold, silver, and beautiful jewels back to Spain from the rich New World—America.

Little do the Spanish sailors know, but on the other side of the island, another ship is waiting. It is a pirate ship!

As long as there have been ships to carry treasure across the seas, there have been pirate ships to rob them.

This pirate captain has a plan. He will trick the Spanish ship. He raises a Spanish flag and slowly steers his ship into view. The Spanish captain thinks the ship is friendly, so he does not sail away.

When the pirates are close enough to the Spanish ship, the pirate captain calls to his men, "Hoist the Jolly Roger!"

A black-and-white flag slides up the mast, and the Spanish sailors panic. The flag is a signal. "We are pirates!" it says. "Surrender or be sorry!"

The skull and crossed swords on the flag show that this ship belongs to greedy "Calico Jack" Rackham. Other pirates had their own special Jolly Rogers, too.

The Spanish ship starts firing, but the pirates fire back with cannonballs and smoke bombs.

The pirate ship is smaller and faster and carries more guns. Does the slow, heavy Spanish galleon stand a chance?

No! Soon two cannonballs chained together fly through the air. They break the big mast of the galleon in two. Now the Spanish sailors cannot even sail away.

The pirates swing ropes with hooks onto the deck and quickly climb aboard.

They are a colorful and frightening sight, waving sharp cutlasses and dressed in bright silk scarves, silver buckles, gold, and jewels—all taken from other sailors on other ships.

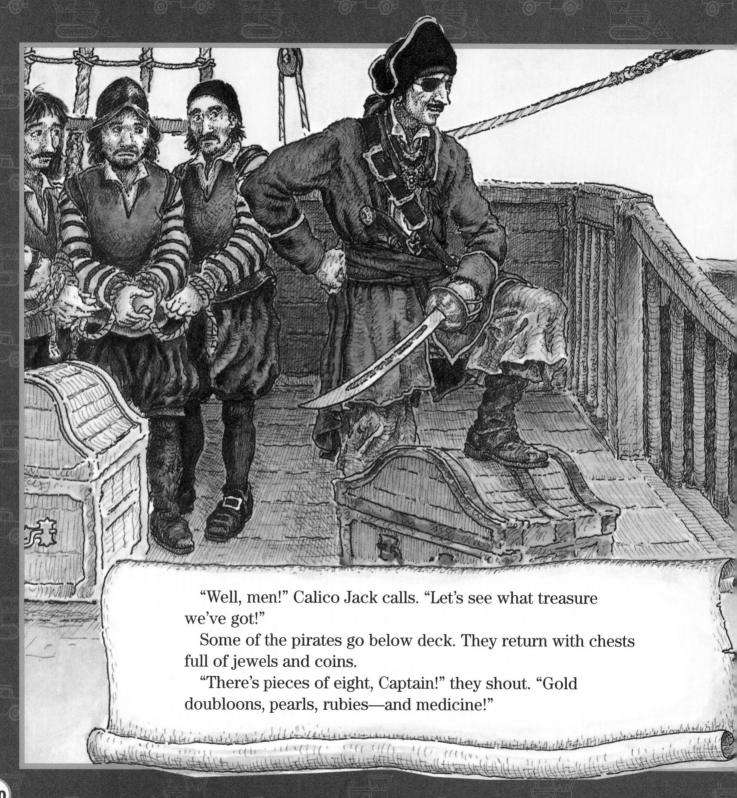

"Well, men!" Calico Jack calls. "Let's see what treasure we've got!"

Some of the pirates go below deck. They return with chests full of jewels and coins.

"There's pieces of eight, Captain!" they shout. "Gold doubloons, pearls, rubies—and medicine!"

Money and jewels are not the only kinds of treasure the pirates are after. They have been at sea for a very long time, and some are sick and hungry. To them, food and medicine are as valuable as gold.

The pirates take all they can from the ship, and burn what they can't carry. Then they sail away to divide up the loot. Each pirate gets an equal share—except for the captain, who gets more. It is part of the pirates' code.

Although they were thieves and murderers, many pirate crews made up their own strict laws to live by. Some even wrote them down. This is how one pirate code might have looked.

Code of Conduct

All crew members shall get an equal share of treasure.

The captain shall get twice as much.

The captain shall be elected fairly.

Everyone shall have an equal vote.

No gambling aboard ship.

While at sea, lanterns and candles must be out at eight o'clock.

Stealing from crewmates and deserting will be punished.

If a pirate broke his ship's code, he was punished. For a small crime, like gambling, a pirate might be fined. But a pirate who did something worse, such as stealing from his shipmates, was in big trouble! Then he was marooned—he was taken to a deserted island and left there with nothing but a jug of water.

What did a pirate do when he was not robbing ships and counting up his loot? He waited at sea for the next ship to rob! Sometimes he waited for weeks and weeks. Then a pirate's life was pretty boring.

Most of the time was spent repairing the ship—patching up ripped sails and mending the lines. The pirates also had to catch their dinner. If they didn't find any fish, they would have to eat hard, wormy biscuits and warm beer.

The best time for pirates came *after* they had robbed a ship.
Then they returned to shore to celebrate. Port Royal, Jamaica,
was one of the favorite hangouts of the pirates of the Caribbean.

There they ate and drank, gambled and acted as wild as they could, until their treasure was spent and it was time to steal some more.

Of course, not all pirates spent every bit of their loot. The famous pirate Blackbeard is said to have buried lots of his treasure. He was going to come back for it later, but he was captured before he could.

Blackbeard's real name was Edward Teach, and he was one of the meanest pirates ever to set sail. His long, black, bushy beard was tied up with colored ribbons. He wore six pistols, and if that didn't make him look fierce enough, he stuck long matches under his hat and set them on fire to make himself look more frightening.

Many treasure hunters have searched for Blackbeard's hidden loot, but no one has ever found it.

Other pirates are said to have buried treasure, too. One of the most famous is Captain Kidd. They say he buried his fortune somewhere on Gardiner's Island, near Long Island, New York, almost three hundred years ago.

The pirate Benito Bonito of the Bloody Sword also left behind a treasure. Today it is called the Lost Loot of Lima. Some say it is still buried on an island off South America. The island's nickname is "Treasure Island." But that fortune, too, has never been found.

There are many more pirate stories. There is even one about a ship made up only of women, which sailed around the Baltic Sea eight hundred years ago.

The captain was a Swedish princess named Alwilda. When her father ordered her to marry a prince she did not love, she ran away to sea and became the leader of an all-woman pirate crew.

Usually, women weren't allowed on pirate ships. But there were two women in Calico Jack's crew. Anne Bonny and Mary Read dressed up in men's clothes so that neither their prisoners nor their shipmates would know who they really were.

When Calico Jack finally discovered he had women on his crew, he kept their secret, too. Anne and Mary were two of his bravest pirates, and he did not want to lose them.

Today, ships still carry treasure across the oceans, but they are much faster and stronger now, and have better ways of guarding their riches. Luckily, the dangerous days of pirates are over. Still, everyone loves to hear stories about the wild robbers of the seas.

COWBOYS

By Lucille Recht Penner
Illustrated by Ben Carter

If you were out west about a hundred years ago,
you might have heard a cowboy yelling—
ti yi yippy yay!—as he rode across the plains.
    What was it like to be a cowboy way back then?

Cowboys lived on cattle ranches. A ranch had a house for the rancher and his family, barns for animals, and a bunkhouse where the cowboys slept. The rancher owned thousands of cattle. They wandered for miles looking for grass and water.

Twice a year, the cowboys drove all the cattle together. This was called a roundup. The cowboys counted the baby calves that had been born since the last roundup. The biggest cattle were chosen to sell at market.

A roundup was hard work. The cattle were wild and fast. They had long, sharp, dangerous horns. Cowboys called them Longhorns. If you made a Longhorn mad, it would charge at you. A cowboy didn't want to get close to an angry Longhorn.

So he made a loop in the end of his rope. Then he twirled it over his head and let it fly. When he caught the Longhorn, he could tell that it belonged to his ranch.

How could he tell? It was easy. Each rancher put a special mark called a brand on his cows. Baby calves didn't have brands, yet. They didn't need them. A baby calf always followed its mother.

Every ranch had its own name and its own brand. The Rocking Chair Ranch brand looked like a rocking chair. The Flying V Ranch brand looked like this: ᴠ

After the roundup was over, it was time to sell the Longhorns. That meant taking them to big market towns. Back then, there were no roads across the wide plains—only dusty trails that cattle had made with their hooves as they tramped along. Some trails were a thousand miles long! Since cattle could walk only fifteen miles a day, the long, hard trip often lasted months. It was called a trail drive. There was a lot to do to get ready.

At the beginning of a trail drive, one cowboy rode out in front of the herd. "Come on, boys," he called to the cattle. A few big Longhorns started after him. They bellowed and swung their heads from side to side. Other cattle followed, and soon they were all on their way.

Cattle didn't like so much walking. After a while, they wanted to turn around and go home. Cowboys rode up and down the sides of the herd to keep them in line. A few cowboys rode at the end of the herd to make sure no cattle were left behind.

It was hot on the trail. Cowboys wore hats with wide brims to keep the sun out of their eyes. When it rained, the brims made good umbrellas. Around their necks, cowboys wore red bandannas. When it got dusty, they pulled the bandannas over their noses. Leather leggings—called chaps—were tied over their pants to keep out thorns and cactus spines.

High leather books kept out dirt and pebbles. Cowboy boots had handles called "mule ears." The cowboy grabbed the mule ears to pull his boots off and on.

What else did a cowboy need on the trail? A good horse. Cowboys spent the whole day on horseback. They rode little horses called cow ponies. A good cow pony was fearless. It could cross rough ground in the blackest night. It could swim a deep, wide river.

It could crash right through the bushes after a runaway cow.
The cowboy had to hold on tight!

Every day the herd tramped the hot, dry plains. Two or three big steers were the leaders. They always walked in front. The cowboys got to know them well. They gave them pet names, like "Old Grumpy" and "Starface."

Cows could get in trouble. Sometimes one got stuck in the mud. The cowboy roped it and pulled it out. A cow might get hurt on the trail. A cowboy took care of that, too.

At night the cowboys stopped to let the cattle eat, drink, and sleep. It was time for the cowboys to eat, too. "Cookie" had a hot meal ready for them. That's what cowboys called the cook.

Cookie drove a special wagon called the chuckwagon. It had drawers for flour, salt, beans, and pots and pans. A water barrel was tied underneath.

Cookie gave every cowboy a big helping of biscuits, steak, gravy, and beans. He cooked the same meal almost every night, but the cowboys didn't mind. It tasted good!

There were no tables or chairs, so the cowboys sat right on the ground. After dinner they played cards or read by the flickering light of the campfire. The nights were chilly and bright with stars.

But the cowboys didn't stay up late. There were tired. At bedtime, they just pulled off their boots and crawled into their bedrolls. A cowboy never wore pajamas. What about a pillow? He used his saddle.

Trail drives were dangerous. Many things could go wrong.
The herd might stampede if there was a loud noise—like a
sudden crash of thunder. A stampede was scary. Cattle ran
wildly in all directions, rolling their eyes and bellowing with
fear. The ground shook under them. The bravest cowboys
galloped to the front of the herd. They had to make the leaders
turn. They shouted at them and fired their six-shooters in the
air. They tried to make the cattle run in a circle until they
calmed down.

Sometimes they'd run into rustlers. A rustler was a cow thief. Rustlers hid behind rocks and jumped out at the cattle to make them stampede. While the cowboys were trying to catch the terrified cattle and calm them down, the rustlers drove off as many as they could.

When the herd came to a big river, the cowboys in front galloped right into the water. The cattle plunged in after them. The cattle swam mostly under water. Sometimes the cowboys could see only the tips of their black noses and their long white horns.

Most cowboys didn't know how to swim. If a cowboy fell into the water, he grabbed his horse's tail and held on tight until they reached shore.

Trail drives often went through Indian Territory. The Indians charged ten cents a head to let the cattle cross their land. If the cowboys didn't pay, there might be a fight. But usually the money was handed over and the herd plodded on.

At last, the noisy, dusty cattle stamped into a market town. The cowboys drove them into pens near the railroad tracks. Then they got their pay. It was time for fun!

What do you think most cowboys wanted first? A bath! The barber had a big tub in the back of the shop. For a dollar, you could soak and soak. A boy kept throwing in pails of hot water. Ahh-h-h! Next it was time for a shave, a haircut, and some new clothes.

Tonight, the cowboys would sleep in real beds and eat dinner at a real table. They would sing, dance, and have fun with their friends.

But soon they would be heading back to Longhorn country. There would be many more hot days in the saddle. There would be many more cold nights under the stars.